AT CHRISTMASTIME

poems by VALERIE WORTH

Michael di Capua Books · HarperCollins Publishers

pictures by ANTONIO FRASCONI

With love to my grown-up children
V.W.

For Luisa Marie Frasconi
A.F.

Early December

When days
Grow short
And bitter,

The drab
Streets, the
Bleak yards,

The bare
Bushes wait—
Not for

Spring, but
Something sooner,
And better.

Winter Dusk

Thin frozen
Rose, veined
Black with
Silent twigs,

Now slowly
Deepening
To breathless
Violet:

While out of
Nowhere blooms
A white
Astounding star.

Wreaths

The glossy
Circles of
Pine and holly
Hung on
A hundred
Doors

Can't outshine
One faded
Cellophane
Hoop
In an upstairs
Window.

Light String

Spread out on
The floor to
Be tested,

All scrawny wire
And cold
Mechanical glass,

There isn't a
Hint of how,
Plugged in,

It glows
Alive—a
Luminous vine,

Lush with
The fruits
Of paradise.

Tree Lot

Weary of glare
And clatter,
Slush and exhaust,

We stop for breath
In this hushed
Miraculous grove,

Haunted by scents
Of distant
Forests and hills

And a ghostly
Unforgettable
Savor of happiness.

Tinsel

Not just its
Glistening furs
Draped over the
Tree's dark fingers,

Or its crisp
Garlands of frost
Looped across every
Warm shop window,

Nor even its sparks
Of ice in the
Prickly halos
Of school angels,

But its whisper
When lifted,
A sifting of
Silks and snows,

And its name,
Holding the faint
Silver tingle of its
Bristles: *tinsel*.

Ornaments

The boxes break
At the corners,
Their sides
Sink weak;

They are tied up
Every year
With the same
Frayed string;

But the split lids
Shelter a hoard
Of treasure: globes
Of gorgeous crystal,

Glittering spires
And bells, jeweled
Nightingales with
Pearly tails.

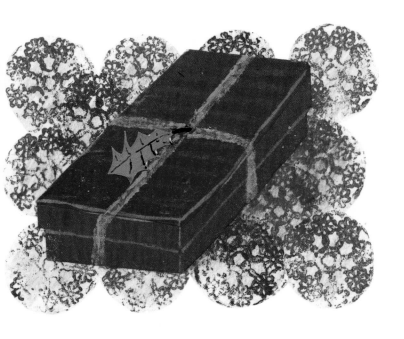

Candy Cane

Hot wintry
Mint, striped
Round with
Fire and snow,

Sweet icicle
That melts
And burns
And chills,

And fills
The mouth with
Fumes of frost
And flame,

Crackling cold
On the tongue,
Like the word
Christmas.

Wrappings

The plainest
Underwear, the
Homeliest socks,

Parceled in
Golden foil and
Silver string,

Or even in flimsy
Red-and-green
Poinsettias,

Become the
Sumptuous offerings
Of a king.

Christmas Tree

Winter and
Darkness
Wither before
Its splendor:

Its branches
Brave with
Fiery lamps
And orbs,

Its bold
Flourish of life
In the dead
Of December.

Decorations

It's odd how
The lofty mansion
Shows only a
Couple of candles
And a modest
Evergreen spray,

While the humble
Bungalow boasts
Lights galore, a
Foil front door,
A life-size
Santa and sleigh.

Crèche

The sheep
Tend to
Fall over,

The angel
Is lacking
A wing;

Even the
Baby looks
Shabby—

So that
It's hard
To explain

Their sturdy
Abiding
Beauty.

Christmas Eve

The tree left
Dim and fragrant,
Guarded by gifts,

The house made
Ready, everything
Tidy and tight;

Even the sky
Held rapt, a poise
Of diamond dark,

A glimmering stillness,
Waiting to greet
The light.

Wise Men

Crossing that
Southerly desert
Of bleached and
Waterless sand,

Their dusty
Camels seem
To move among
Drifts of snow,

Under a high
Blue dome of
Shivering stars
As cold as ours.

Angels

Watching from
Heaven, they
Float on the
Spangled air:

The great
Sheaves of
Plumage at
Their shoulders

Serenely folded,
One long
Gleaming feather
Over another.

Santa Claus

Santa Claus is
In the wind:
Sweeping out
Of north skies
Furred with snow,
Slipping along
Red-berried byways
All the gray
Day, sailing all
Night through
The moon-clear
Dark: his
Breath bright
Frost, his eyes
Thrilling stars,
His vast hands
Spilling gold
Fires down every
Black chimney.

Christmas Morning

Those presents
We planted
Last night
At the foot
Of the tree

Have sprouted
And spread
To a flowering
Field of
Surprises.

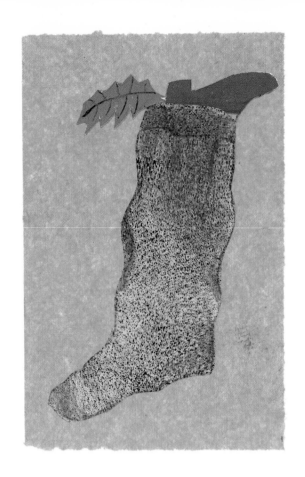

Stockings

Long ago, we
Hung up my
Mother's old

Nylons, and
Woke to find
Them swollen

With beige
Unnatural bulges,
Thigh to toe.

Nowadays, there
Are velvety
Crimson boots,

Brighter, and
Shapelier—but
A lot shorter.

Cat Toys

There's always
A ball or
A mouse,

Lovingly
Wrapped
And given,

Received
With gracious
Attention:

But the real
Success is
The ribbon.

Presents

Maybe
Pushed under
The rug,

Or hidden
Behind
A chair,

Or handed
To somebody
Else—

Isn't there
Just one
More?

Three O'clock

This afternoon
The Christmas tree

Stands wanly in
A sunny window,

Its flashy
Nightly jollity

Diminished to a
Melancholy glister.

Christmas Dinner

A moment of
Flickering magic
Touches the
Crowded table,

Lending invisible
Halos to
Aunt and baby
And granny,

Casting a silent
Glory over the
Turkey and
Cranberry jelly.

Christmas Night

It seemed the
Gloomiest hour
Of all the year,

Until my father
Took me out
To walk across

A quiet field
Beneath a sky
Of indigo,

The woods asleep,
The stars
Beginning to appear.

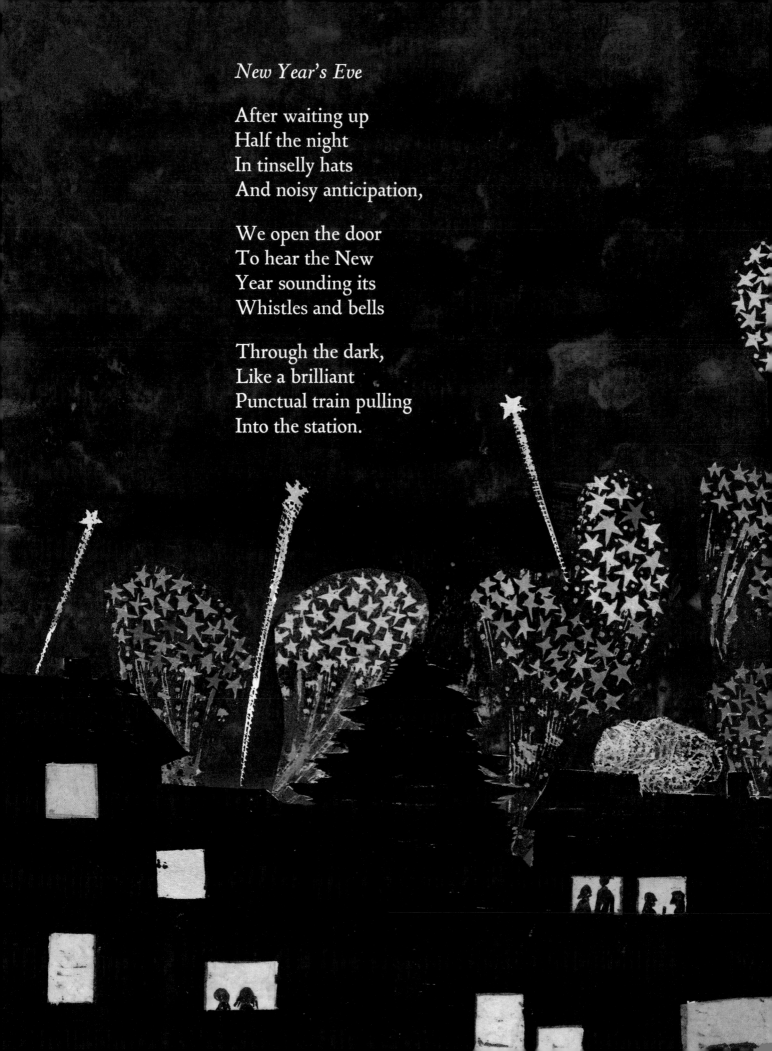

New Year's Eve

After waiting up
Half the night
In tinselly hats
And noisy anticipation,

We open the door
To hear the New
Year sounding its
Whistles and bells

Through the dark,
Like a brilliant
Punctual train pulling
Into the station.

New Year's Day

Now the luster
Of Christmas
Pales, its
Luxury stales,
Its wrappings
And trappings
Dwindle to
Empty show.

Time to
Consider the
World afresh,
To tidy away
The gaudy
Trash, to
Study the
Sober snow.

Tree Fire

Chopped for
The hearth,
Touched with
A match,
And gone
In a blaze
Of farewells,

It rushes
Rejoicing
Up the dark
Flue, spinning
Its final
Radiance back
To the sun.

Twelfth Night

Houses veil
Their barren
Windows,

Streets
Hold only
Traffic lights;

Red paper
Bells at the
Drugstore

Suddenly
Turn into
Valentines.

Carols

In January
They wane
To tinny jingles;

But they'll
Be back again
By next November,

With every
Note a peal
Of soulful silver.

Spring

In spring, the old
Driveway snowdrifts
Shrink to a row
Of polished puddles;

Over the wet
Black road slender
Spokes of bicycles
Blink and sparkle;

By the muddy path
Glints a single
Crumpled strand
Of Christmas tinsel.